Arthur the Fly-Slayer
& the Forty Dragons

May my family's fairy tale

grow on you with every reading.

Maria Kamoulakou

For kids' activities please visit:

www.mariakamoulakou.com

LITTLE CENTAUR PRESS

THANK YOU for your purchase.
We would greatly appreciate your
review on Amazon.com

Arthur
the Fly-Slayer

& the Forty Dragons

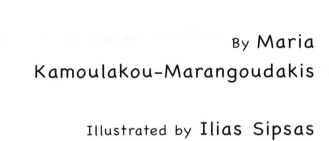

By Maria
Kamoulakou–Marangoudakis

Illustrated by Ilias Sipsas

Published by LITTLE CENTAUR PRESS
795 S. Branch Pkwy, Springfield, Massachusetts 01118
www.littlecentaurpress.com
littlecentaurpress@yahoo.com

Printed in Canada by Marquis Imprimeur Inc.
First printing December 2018

ISBN: 978-1-7324758-0-9

Library of Congress Control Number: 2018907328

Illustrations: Ilias Sipsas

Kitten drawings by the author

Graphic design: Ina Melengoglou - altsys.gr

Cover design: Ilias Sipsas & Ina Melengoglou

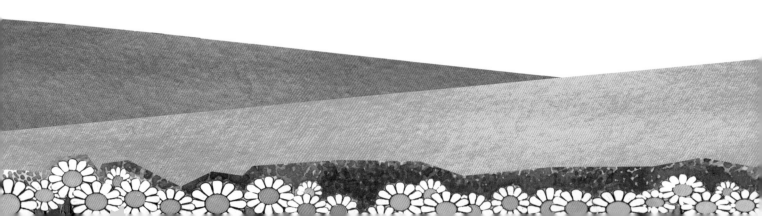

Did your father ever tell you fairy tales? Mine did! The nights I was in bed with a cold, he comforted me with a Spartan fairy tale he heard from his grandmother. Naturally, I knew the story by heart! Yet, I anxiously anticipated his return from work only to listen to it again, and to correct him at the end… You could say that my father's narration of the Forty Dragons tale was second best only to missing school! This is my own version of the tale. Enjoy and feel free to add to it with your imagination…

Dedicated to my beloved father Theodoros,

his mother Eleftheria and

her mother Stavroula

Table of contents

Pump the wheel to spin...

The old chair creaked loudly as Granny sat down at the spinning wheel by the fireplace. The sound of distant giggles and pounding feet that grew louder and louder made her smile. Before Granny had a chance to fix her apron, her grandchildren stormed into the room, their cheeks rosy from running. They swarmed around her like little bees, pushing one another as they took their usual places on the wooden floor. Whenever their grandmother sat at the spinning wheel, the children knew it was story time. Disturbed by the sudden commotion, a couple of kittens sneaked under Granny's long skirt for protection and comfort.

"Shhhhhhhhhhhhhhh," Granny said, demanding silence by resting her finger gently against her lips. All eyes were now set on her. She pulled the yarn basket closer to her feet and, with a gentle pump at the foot treadle of the spinning wheel, Granny began to spin wool. Using both hands she spun woolen threads with swift and confident movements, creating yarn that wrapped around a bobbin.

The kittens purred happily under Granny's skirt, and playfully pawed the hem of her petticoat. The wood gently crackled in the fireplace. A sudden burst of sparks shot like fireworks towards Granny's feet and momentarily startled her audience. The scene was now set for a magical evening in the dim light of the fireplace and the soothing comfort of the fire.

"Tie the yarn to the bobbin," said Granny. "Pump the wheel to spin, and let our story begin..."

The village

Once upon a time there was a blacksmith who lived with his family in a small but tidy village at the fringes of a fertile plain. Most of his fellow villagers were farmers and shepherds with large herds of sheep and goats. They all enjoyed a quiet and peaceful life. They dwelled in well-built stone houses with thatched roofs and had spacious gardens filled with colorful flowers and fragrant herbs. Children roamed the streets, playing games that came down to them through the ages. Their carefree laughter echoed down cobblestone streets and dirt alleys.

A colorful patchwork of fields surrounded the village. Fields yellow with wheat and snow-white with fluffy cotton. Fields green with beans and bright red with juicy tomatoes. Fruit trees loaded with oranges, lemons, cherries and figs were kept in orchards of all shapes and sizes.

The villagers were particularly proud of their olive trees; the most noble of all trees! Every other year, the branches curved towards the ground, heavy with fruit. During harvest, large nets were laid out under the trees to collect the olives as they ripened and fell. Some were kept for eating and the rest were crushed into olive oil. This precious oil was used in cooking, to make perfumes and soaps, but most importantly, to light up people's houses with oil lamps. There was no waste! Even the crushed pits and skins were burned, in place of charcoal, to heat up people's homes in winter.

The olive tree is a truly blessed tree. It can live for hundreds or thousands of years without failing to offer its crops. The leaves have a dark and a lighter side.

With every gust of the wind, the olive groves turn from sage green to silvery ash like a chameleon changes color.

"Does anyone remember who offered the first olive tree to mankind?" Granny paused and stared over her tiny, round glasses.

"Yes! I do!" Yiannis jumped up with excitement. Of all her grandchildren he was the one who loved talking to an audience. "In Greek mythology it was Athena, the Goddess of wisdom, who offered the olive tree as a present to the city of Athens."

"Well done, Yiannis!" Granny said and smiled. "And what else?"

"The olive tree became a symbol of peace and prosperity," added Yiannis, boasting like a peacock.

"Its branches were used to make wreaths that crowned the winning athletes during the ancient Olympic Games, in place of gold, silver, and bronze medals."

"We all know that, Yiannis! Sit down!" interrupted Anna, the eldest of the grandchildren. "Could you please go on with the story, Granny?"

"Of course, my children," remarked Granny and she continued her storytelling.

Several little stores were built around the central square of the village. The most popular was the bakery, where fresh bread and cookies were baked every day. Close to the fresh water spring stood the potter's hut. He skillfully molded large chunks of wet clay into elegant cups and dishes, and then fired them in an outdoor brick oven. Another shop at the heart of the village was the tannery, where the shoemaker fashioned custom-made shoes out of soft leather hides. Finally, close to the tannery stood the forge. Day in and day out, the blacksmith heated, hammered, and shaped metal rods into nails, agricultural tools, horseshoes, and swords.

The blacksmith had three daughters, Mara, Niki and Antonia, and a younger son, Arthur. Back in those days, it was customary for boys to help their father and learn his trade, while the girls did housework and looked after their younger siblings. The blacksmith's daughters helped their mother daily in the kitchen. They washed clothes in the river and collected kindling for the stove. They even fetched water from the spring in large ceramic jugs which they skillfully balanced on their heads.

Every morning, a similar scene was repeated in the blacksmith's household. The only things that changed were the tasks and the names.

"Mara, pick up the laundry basket and go wash the clothes, please," ordered their mother. Nikki and Antonia giggled and made faces at Mara behind their mother's back.

"Why me, Mama? I washed the clothes last week! Why not Nikki or Antonia?" protested Mara, thumping her feet on the ground.

"Because your silly little sisters are going to fetch kindling and fill the jars with water for cooking. When they are done with giggling, that is," added their mother turning sharply to face her two daughters.

"Arthur?" shouted the blacksmith as he galloped down the stairs and entered the kitchen in a hurry. "Where is Arthur? Has he gone to the forge yet?" he asked his wife.

"He wasn't in his bed when I got up," she replied, raising her eyebrows and shaking her head. "Here, sit down. Let me make you some breakfast." She dragged a chair away from the table.

"No time for breakfast, my dear. I need to run," responded the blacksmith. He grabbed a piece of soft cheese and a slice of bread on his way out and mumbled, "Off to work!"

The blacksmith's son

The blacksmith's son, Arthur, was somewhat of a daydreamer. Every day he looked for excuses to escape from the stifling hot forge and relax in the breezy coolness of the nearby woods. Working by his father's side was very demanding. Every morning he woke up early and ran to the forge to light the furnace. Once the flames had begun to roar, he rolled up his sleeves, tied a leather apron behind his waist, and fetched freezing cold water from the spring in large buckets. Then, he tidied up the forge, inspected the tools and carried firewood for the furnace.

Day in and day out, Arthur watched his father shape blazing hot pieces of metal into all sorts of useful objects and learned the trade. The blacksmith held the pieces firmly with large metal tongs against a metal surface called an anvil and beat them hard with a huge hammer. The deep, dull sound of the hammer echoed like a symphony of church bells in Arthur's ears!

It was no surprise that at every given opportunity, Arthur sneaked into the forest and took short naps in the shade of the tall pine trees. During his leisurely escapes, he frequently daydreamed of being a knight in shining armor fighting ferocious warriors, or combating dangerous thieves and scary dragons.

In the summer months, Arthur's naps were constantly interrupted by pestering, buzzing flies. No swatter would keep them away!
And then one day, he had enough.

"I am sick of you little, pestering, good-for-nothing insects!" he fumed out loud, feverishly swinging his arms in front of his face.

There and then, he decided to forge himself a long and wide sword to slay them all with a single swipe.

"Beware flies! You will soon meet your master!" he exclaimed, and he ran swiftly back to the forge.

For several weeks, Arthur sweated over his sword. He stayed behind every evening after his father had finished working. First, he heated the blade in the fire. Then he hammered it on the anvil with steady rhythmical movements, releasing sparks like firecrackers with every blow. The cycle of heating and hammering the blade was repeated endlessly for days. Three weeks later, when he was satisfied with his work, he dipped the blade in cold water to harden it. Then he carved a wooden handle and wrapped it with a thick leather cord for a better grip.

Now that I am done, let's see how many of you will survive my deadly blows, he thought with a smirk, as he admired the quality of his work.

The next day, Arthur was eager to test his blade on the flies. He ran into the forest and lay down under his favorite tree. He remained still until the familiar buzzing sound drilled into his ears, like a woodpecker drills holes into the trees.

"Buzzzzzzzzzzzzzz…," then silence.

With swift decisive swipes, one fly after another met its fate, swirling down like tiny twisters before littering the ground around Arthur's pointy-toed shoes. By the next morning, there was no trace of them. A long trail of tiny ants had carried away the dead flies to their underground quarters and stored them for winter.

Now there is a good use for those pestering insects, he thought.

After Arthur had killed hundreds and hundreds of flies, the villagers jokingly gave him the nickname "Arthur the Fly-Slayer". His father was terribly embarrassed by this, but Arthur was so proud of his deeds that, in reply to this teasing, he inscribed the following verse on his sword:

At rest I slay forty. Beware when I rise!

When Arthur rested in the forest, his trusty sword always lay by his side, with the inscribed side facing up, readily available to make short work of any insect that disturbed his sleep.

An unexpected encounter

One day, while Arthur was fast asleep under a pine tree by the main road, two weary travelers paused close to him to get out of the hot, blazing sun and to catch their breath. They were a father and son from a remote village on the other side of the forest, several days' walk away.

"I am so hot, tired, and hungry," complained the son, rubbing his empty stomach as it rumbled like thunder.

"Bear with me, son," answered the father. He dried his sweaty forehead with the back of his palm. "There is a village on the horizon. We will rest there and gather information for our journey."

"Is there someone sleeping under those trees?"

"Where?"

"Look! Over there. By the sharp turn in the road," added the son, pointing in Arthur's direction with his walking cane. "He seems to be a warrior. There is a sword by his side."

"Be careful, son. Best keep alert. He could be a bandit."

The two travelers tiptoed towards Arthur with great caution, for fear of waking him up. The inscription on Arthur's sword glittered in the sun and they bent down to read it.

At rest I slay forty. Beware when I rise!

"Our good fellow! It is *you* we have been searching for!" exclaimed the father in great delight. "You are our man!"

"Yippeeee! This is the end of our quest. We can go home now," cried the son, jumping up and down with joy.

Arthur, woken up by all the commotion, was confused and perplexed. Between yawning and rubbing his eyes, he heard the strangers rambling about forty terrible dragons that were venturing out at night and storming their village. The dragons would steal their cattle, trample their fields with their clumsy feet, and eat the fruit from their trees. They would even steal wine and olive oil from their barns. The villagers were desperately looking for a brave warrior to chase the dragons away and save their village from misery and starvation. In exchange, they offered a chest of gold coins and a position on the village council!

"Where exactly did you say that you're from?" asked Arthur as he slowly stood up.

"We come from Keeta, a small village on the other side of the dark forest. Beyond the Three Sisters," replied the son,

pointing his walking cane at three shining mountain peaks on the horizon behind them.

The prospect of an adventure was very tempting and Arthur did not hesitate.

"Maybe I *am* your man!" remarked Arthur, raising his left eyebrow.

Quite sure of himself, he stood up and led the travelers to his village. Back in those days it was customary to offer shelter, food, and wine to weary travelers and strangers who showed up at the door. The blacksmith's family welcomed the two men and, according to custom, offered them a hot meal and a bed in which to rest their aching bodies.

The next morning, by the time the two travelers woke up, Arthur had already prepared for the journey. The blacksmith feared the worst and tried to dissuade him, but all was in vain. Arthur would not hear a word!

"Are you out of your mind going after forty dragons?

You don't stand a chance, my boy. Killing one dragon is hard enough, let alone forty…," pleaded the blacksmith in despair.

"Don't worry, Father," Arthur reassured him, resting one hand on his shoulder. "I will be just fine."

Don't worry? thought the blacksmith. He looked straight into his son's eyes. "You have absolutely no idea what danger you are putting yourself into. You are no warrior, Arthur!" he exclaimed, stressing every single word.

"You are just a simple blacksmith," his father continued. "You don't stand a chance, my son. Please have pity on us. Think of your mother and sisters, who haven't stopped weeping since they heard the news. One day you will be the head of

this family. Who will look after them when I am gone if anything happens to you?" he pleaded.

"But I have my sword, Father. It is the sharpest and swiftest blade in the village! Besides, everybody knows that despite their large size and supernatural strength, dragons are as dumb as turkeys. It shouldn't be that hard to outsmart them."

Having said that, Arthur threw a hand-woven bag containing a few clothes and a flask of water over his shoulder, hung the sword from his belt, and moved straight for the front door. On the kitchen table he noticed a basket with his favorite delicacy: soft white cheese made from goat's milk. Fresh and juicy! His mother had just finished shaping it into flat pieces like large pebbles, and the milk was still dripping from the basket. Arthur grabbed a piece, wrapped it in paper, and put it in his pocket. He escorted the travelers out of the house and headed straight for the woods.

His father's voice echoed behind them: "Remember to look back at the trail and memorize your way home…"

Into the woods

For several hours, the travelers followed mountain paths that Arthur had never taken before. The pine forest behind his village soon gave way to a mixed forest of tall maple trees and nut trees heavy with shells. Chestnuts in their prickly hedgehog shells littered their path and tiny acorns bounced off their heads. The walnut trees were heavy with green velvety shells that hadn't burst open yet. Red squirrels chased one another, jumping from branch to branch over Arthur's head with great precision, like acrobats in a circus. Forest birds tweeted their afternoon songs and hares hopped to safety at the first sight of the travelers. A deer swiftly disappeared into the bushes in the distance.

Arthur snapped branches along the way, hoping they would lead him on his return. He followed his father's advice to frequently look over his shoulder and notice specific landmarks. With every glance at the trail behind them, Arthur tried to memorize specific features that would help him find his way back: an oak tree struck by lightning, a huge rock, a dry streambed, a sudden turn of the trail.

 "Where are we going exactly?" demanded Arthur as the forest became denser and darker. The fertile deciduous trees had now been replaced by towering cedar trees that pierced the sky. As the winding trail led them deeper into the woods, a light fog, like fluffy white cotton candy, descended from the mountains and covered the treetops.

"We are taking you as close to dragon territory as possible," explained the son. His cheeks were flushed from climbing and from the chilly mountain breeze.

With sore feet and scratched legs, Arthur followed in the footsteps of the two travelers.

"How much longer?" he asked.

"Until we see the footprints of the dragons," replied the father, breathing quickly.

Towards the evening, they reached a clearing in the woods filled with patches of white daisies and numerous muddy holes brimming with rain water and dry leaves.

As Arthur bent down to pluck a daisy, he paused to examine the holes more closely.

What funny looking mud puddles. They almost look like... footprints! he thought, and without hesitation he placed his right foot inside one of the puddles to explore its size and depth.

With a loud SPLASH, his foot sank up to the ankle in muddy water.

Could these be the footprints of the dragons? They look at least twenty sizes bigger than mine!

His stream of thoughts was interrupted by the trembling voices of his terrified companions. The father and son bent over another mud puddle and examined it carefully.

"It is deep," said the son.

"I can make out the outline of a paw with sharp claws," added the father with a trembling voice.

"And the size is right."

"These *are* dragon footprints. There is no doubt about it," confirmed the father, shaking with fear.

I wonder how much dragons weigh, Arthur thought, scratching his head as he lifted his foot from the muddy water.

"We have definitely entered the territory of the forty dragons," declared the son, and like a startled deer he looked frantically over his shoulders.

"We need to go. Immediately! There is no time to waste," exclaimed the father. And, turning to Arthur, he added "From now on, you are on your own, my boy. Good luck to you!"

"Wait! Don't go yet!" yelled Arthur as they turned around and started running.

The two travelers raced like bunny rabbits out of the clearing, leaping over rocks and mud. Suddenly, Arthur was left behind, all by himself, in the stillness of the woods.

The forty dragons

It is said that dragons have the ability to smell humans from miles away, and it wasn't long before the earth began to shake. At first, Arthur felt a distant, rhythmic pounding.

"They are coming!" he whispered to himself.

With remarkable calmness, he lay down against a tree, placing the sword by his side. He gently bit the white daisy, twisting it a few times between his teeth, and lowered the hat over his eyes, pretending to be asleep.

I am ready now, he reassured himself, *let them come.*

As the dragons drew closer, the ground shook and the woods shivered. With every step, dry leaves broke free from the trees and danced their way to the ground.

Before long, the clearing was filled with huge, scary creatures that looked very much like gigantic lizards. There were forty of them, all bright red, with long crocodile snouts, pointy white teeth and eyes that sparkled like diamonds.

Their leader, Ulof the Cunning, approached Arthur with the confidence of a lion stalking its prey. Arthur felt the dragon's warm, stinking breath on his face as Ulof the Cunning bent over the sword and read the inscription out loud.

At rest I slay forty. Beware when I rise!

"Ahhhhhhh!" exclaimed the dragons in unison. Their leader stumbled a few steps back, flapping his tiny wings in distress. Alarmed, he led the forty dragons back into the dark cover of the woods in several giant leaps.

"This despicable human brags that he can kill forty of us!" he said to his companions.

"Nonsense! Who would dare confront us?" whispered one dragon.

"He is only human. His strength does not compare to ours," added a second one.

"Come on, boys, let's kill him while he is still asleep," suggested a third one, encouraging the dragons to approach Arthur.

Taking clumsy steps and swinging their tails like dinosaurs, the forty dragons closed in on Arthur from all sides. The dragons' eyes were sparkling bright, their teeth shining, and their claws ready to strike.

To their surprise, Arthur grabbed his sword and swiftly jumped up to face them, like the knight in his daydreams. He took a large step forward, bent his knee and thrust his sword in the direction of those who were closest to him. He shouted angrily, "This is *my* forest and you are trespassing on *my* private property. You steal *my* animals and feed on *my* fruit and vegetables." As Arthur jumped up, he felt something slip from his pocket. It was the piece of fresh cheese that he had taken from his mother's basket earlier in the day.

At first, the dragons were startled by Arthur's reaction, but it didn't take long before their leader stepped forward in a threatening manner.

"All this time, we have never seen you in this part of the woods," he said to Arthur with a wicked smile, exposing a single line of dirty, sharp teeth. "The forest belongs to *us* now. We are many and we are stronger than you, so you'd better collect your things and move on." He showed Arthur the way out of the clearing with his pointy claw.

"Yes, I can see that you are many, but your strength does not compare to mine," Arthur replied, unafraid. He stood tall, in defiance of the dragons, and blew the hair from his eyes before continuing. "I challenge you to a contest of physical strength. If the mightiest of you manages to squeeze water out of a stone, then I will leave and the forest will be yours forever. But if I win, then *you* will leave, never to return."

The dragons looked at each other and burst out laughing at the nerve of this young man. This loathsome human amused them so much!

They laughed hysterically, shedding huge tears and holding their bellies. The tall cedar trees shook from their laughter and disturbed the birds that were nesting for the night.

The dragons were so confident of their powers that they accepted the challenge wholeheartedly, but added one condition of their own: Arthur would have to go first.

Arthur agreed without hesitation. The dragons made a circle around Arthur and stepped aside for Drako the Invincible, the strongest of all dragons, to move forward. Then, beating his belly like a drum, Ulof the Cunning ceremonially announced, "Let the contest begin!"

All forty sets of bright eyes watched with curiosity as Arthur bent down, pretending to search for a small stone. Clever as he was, he grabbed instead the piece of fresh cheese that had earlier fallen out of his pocket. He squeezed it hard, again and again, groaning and moaning in a great theatrical performance. Finally, a few drops escaped his tight fist and found their way to the ground with a splash!

The dragons closest to Arthur blinked repeatedly in disbelief. They had just witnessed the impossible. A feeble human had squeezed water out of a stone! They towered over him with suspicion and mistrust, but there were clearly a few drops of water on the ground. There was no disputing it. The dragons who were further away pushed closer to take a peek.

A low murmur gradually echoed around the clearing.

"What a daring young man!" one of the dragons whispered in admiration and wonder.

"Did you see that? He mashed the stone like a boiled potato!" remarked a second one in fear.

"He is clearly stronger than he looks," added another with widened eyes.

"Absolutely!" agreed a fourth one, nodding his head.

"Appearances can be deceiving. Never judge a human by his looks," remarked Eli the Wise, the eldest of them all.

"Come, come, my friends. Give us some space. Step back and let's continue the contest," interrupted the dragon leader, overshadowing all other comments.

Drako the Invincible bent over and grabbed a white stone from the ground near his feet. Very confident of victory, Drako smirked as the stone disappeared in his tight grip. With the first squeeze, blood rushed to his face and his eyes goggled. He squeezed again and again until blood dripped from his claws and hot white steam came out of his nostrils. The forest shook from his groaning and the birds flew from their nests. Forty sets of diamond eyes were fixed on Drako with anguish and concern. All was in vain! He could not squeeze a single drop of water from the stone. How disappointing!

Drako the Invincible slowly released the stone from his tight grip and lowered his eyes, acknowledging defeat. What an embarrassment in front of the dragon clan! One by one the dragons turned their backs on the contestants and retreated into the woods.

Arthur sighed and blinked with relief. Instinctively his right hand touched the sword. This was no time for celebration. His fate relied on what the dragons would do next.

Seeing his clan in disarray, Ulof the Cunning decided to take matters into his own hands. In his mind, there were two options. They could either honor the agreement and abandon the forest, or somehow get Arthur on their side. Reluctant to leave their feeding grounds, he therefore decided to invite Arthur to live with them. *Befriend your enemy and look for ways to undermine him*, he thought, carefully hiding a wicked smile.

"Young stranger, I know I speak for all when I say that we admire your bravery and strength," announced the leader calmly. "In all our travels, we have never encountered anyone quite like you. We would be honored if you would accept our invitation to join our clan."

Arthur raised his eyebrows in disbelief.

"Consider how rich you could become. With your powers, we would conquer more lands, prosper, and live comfortably until the end of our days," argued Ulof the Cunning.

Arthur was greatly surprised by the dragon's proposal. Living with forty dragons was a scary idea. On the other hand, if he refused to join them then his life would surely be in danger. He decided to accept their offer in order to buy himself time.

"Mighty dragons," he said, looking around at the dragons scattered under the trees. "I will gladly extend my hospitality and live with you in *my* woods. The forest provides plenty of food for all of us. As to the conquering of new lands, it would be best to wait until next summer when the weather is warm and the days are long," he announced with a smile.

The dragons slowly got up and gathered around him. They felt relieved and happy that they wouldn't have to abandon the woods.

"I don't know about you, but I am starving and night is falling. Take me to your home," demanded Arthur.

Ulof the Cunning led the way. Arthur and the forty dragons followed him deeper into the forest, until they reached a dark cave. The huge cave entrance gaped like a hungry mouth on the mountainside.

That night, they all feasted on stolen goat meat and the woods shook from their merry dancing.

The trials

Life with the dragons was not easy. Arthur's abilities were constantly put to the test as Ulof the Cunning sought determinedly to discover his weaknesses. In the weeks following the stone contest, Arthur was sent to do several errands, but resourceful as he was, he managed to avoid any form of hard work.

When Ulof the Cunning told him to gather firewood, Arthur asked for ropes. That night, Arthur and the forty dragons raided the village and collected all the ropes they could find: from barns, tents, and even clothes lines. On the way back to the cave, Arthur once again kept looking over his shoulder and memorizing specific features: a bunch of bare trees, an eagle's nest, a fallen tree, a spring, a steep cliff.

At dawn, Arthur got up before the dragons, tied all the ropes together, threw them over his shoulder, and left the cave in search of firewood. He had a brilliant idea and couldn't wait to put his plan into action.

Back in the cave, the dragons woke up and waited for the firewood. The hours went by, but Arthur was nowhere in sight. Irritated and alarmed by his absence, they decided to leave the cave and look for him.

They did not need to go far. Arthur was close by, holding two ends of the rope in his hands.

"What on earth are you doing?" demanded Ulof the Cunning. "Where is the firewood? How are we going to keep warm inside the cave without a fire?"

"This is it! I've tied up all the trees in the forest and instead of searching for firewood every day, I will bring them all down with a single pull,"

responded Arthur with pride. He took a deep breath, expanding his chest with air like a hot air balloon, and was about to pull both ends of the rope when all the dragons cried out in unison:

"NoNoNoNoNoNooooo!"

They ran towards him in panic.

"Do not spoil our forest!" shouted one.

"Do not destroy our trees!" pleaded another.

"Leave it to us to carry the firewood we need every day!" suggested Ulof the Cunning, and the dragons all scattered in the woods to gather the day's supply.

A few days later, it was Arthur's turn to fetch water from the river. Ulof the Cunning placed a huge leather flask on Arthur's back and asked him to fill it with water. Arthur left the cave moaning and groaning with the weight of the flask as the dragons giggled behind his back, hoping for him to fail.

Hmmmmm! I'd better think fast, or else I am doomed, Arthur thought as he paced towards the river, dragging the flask behind him.

Inside the cave, the dragons waited. The hours went by, but again Arthur was nowhere to be seen. Frustrated and angry, the dragons decided to leave the cave to look for him. Eventually, they found Arthur kneeling by the river, digging a channel with a spoon.

"What on earth are you doing?" demanded Ulof the Cunning. "Have you gone totally mad? Where is the flask with the water? How are we going to cook our favorite stew tonight without water?"

"There is no need to fill the flask," responded Arthur as he slowly got up and shook the dirt off his clothes. "I will dig a channel and simply divert the river to the cave."

He had barely finished his sentence when all the dragons protested in unison:

"NoNoNoNoNoNooooo!"

"Do not divert our river!" pleaded one.

"Without water the villagers will suffer!" said another.

"Their livestock will die, their vegetables will wither, their trees will not bear any fruit," argued a third.

"If this happens, what will be left for us to steal?" wondered Eli the Wise.

"Please leave it to us, Arthur," announced Ulof the Cunning. "Every day we will go and fetch the water that we need." And turning to the strongest of the dragons, "Drako, jump in the river and fill the flask for tonight," he commanded.

As the days became colder, the first snowflakes made their appearance in the woods. From the entrance of the cave, Arthur watched them swiftly flow with the breeze. Like dandelion fluff, they gently landed on tree tops, branches, and fallen leaves. The first brave flakes melted into tiny droplets of crystal clear water. The ones that followed landed in greater numbers, showing determination and persistence. Like frosting on a birthday cake, the woods were soon dressed in white.

During one heavy blizzard, Ulof the Cunning decided to send Arthur hunting, in the secret hope that the treacherous weather would defeat him.

What a great opportunity to get rid of him, once and for all, he thought.

Having no choice in the matter, Arthur made himself a cape by tying several goat hides together, picked up his sword, grabbed his traveling cane, and disappeared into the snowy landscape.

For hours and hours Arthur wandered through the forest until his hands and feet became numb from the blistering cold. There was no sign of life. Squirrels, rabbits, foxes, and deer were safely hidden deep in the woods, avoiding the treacherous weather.

Arthur was beginning to give up all hope when a huge stag caught his eye in the distance. It was leaping through the trees full of pride and grace, completely oblivious to the raging blizzard. Arthur paused and watched him with admiration.

Suddenly, an anguished cry pierced the air. The stag stopped and bellowed. He lifted his head towards the sky and then collapsed heavily on the snow with a loud thump.

What happened? thought Arthur, as he ran to his aid, stumbling through the snow.

The poor creature was already breathing his last. A large bloodstain colored the snow bright red where the stag was laying. Arthur kneeled down and gently caressed the stag's head with tenderness and love. The wounded animal glanced at him in fear and blinked in distress. As the stag gasped his final breath, Arthur watched in disbelief a white butterfly dancing her way to the sky between the falling snowflakes.

My eyes must be playing tricks on me, Arthur thought, and looking down at the stag, *He looks so peaceful now. He is almost smiling!*

It was then that he saw the sharp branch that had sadly claimed his life. Well-hidden into the snow it found its way deep into the stag's belly.

Back in the cave, the dragons had lit a huge fire to keep warm while they waited for Arthur's return. The hours went by and, once again, Arthur was nowhere in sight. With each passing hour the dragons celebrated, thinking that their despicable ally was gone once and for all.

Their leader, Ulof the Cunning, wanted to be sure. So, he dispatched a search party to look for Arthur. With giant leaps the dragons searched the forest, following their acute sense of smell for humans. Eventually Arthur was discovered taking shelter inside a large cavity at the base of a huge tree, all bundled up in his goat cape. The dead stag was lying a few feet away.

"What took you so long?" scolded Arthur. "I hunt for you. I provide meat for your table and all you do is sit around the fire all day long, cleaning your teeth with your claws. Make yourselves useful for once and drag this stag to the cave, because I am starving."

"And one of you had better carry me on his back, because your stride is longer than mine," he ordered in a bossy tone.

The dragons were baffled and disappointed, glancing back and forth between Arthur and the stag. Not only did the boy survive the blizzard, but he had also killed the largest game they had ever seen. They took the shortest way home in silence, their heads lowered like droopy roses. Drako the Invincible dragged the stag behind him, while Eli the Wise carried Arthur on his back.

Ulof the Cunning was not pleased at all to see Arthur alive. However, he hid his disappointment and his dark intentions with false words of praise:

"This is the largest stag I have ever seen! Well done, Arthur! You are truly a mighty hunter. Come and keep warm by the fire while we prepare a feast in your honor."

After roasting the meat over the fire and sitting to feast around the warmth of the central hearth, Arthur and the forty dragons all leaned back against the walls of the cave to digest their delicious meal. The dragons cleaned their teeth with their claws and burped shamelessly loudly with satisfaction.

Inside the secret chamber

That night, the dragons' eyes were fixed on Arthur. All forty pairs of them! It was a dark, mysterious stare that made Arthur feel uneasy and unwelcome. To lighten things up, he needed to do something and fast! Suddenly, an idea came to him; he suggested a drinking contest to warm everyone up from the wintery weather. Predictable as they were, the dragons grabbed their wine goblets with enthusiasm and demanded to be served at once.

Arthur volunteered to fetch the wine jugs. He lit a torch and retreated to the rear of the cave, where the jugs were stored against the walls. As he lowered the torch to look for a jug he could manage to carry, the flame flickered and he felt a cold breeze on his face. Lifting up the torch, he noticed a narrow opening in the wall of the cave. On the spur of the moment, he decided to explore.

Let's see where this leads to, he thought. *It could be a lucky escape in a time of danger.*

Arthur could barely squeeze his slender body through the opening. His clothes scraped against the rocky surface, but he carried on anyway, holding the torch in his right hand. Fortunately, the narrow opening gradually widened, and then it led uphill. Arthur climbed with one hand until he reached a spacious chamber.

"Phew! That was steep!" he murmured, as he raised the torch above his head to take a good look at his surroundings.

Beneath his feet, Arthur could hear the dragons pounding their goblets rhythmically on the ground. He was clearly above them. Exploring the chamber with his torch, he noticed some small openings in the rocky walls.

He took a peek through one of them and immediately smirked as he saw the dragons sitting around the walls of the cave below.

Hmmmmmm, I have an idea, he thought, and smiled. *If it works, we will get rid of the dragons once and for all.*

With the torch in his hand, Arthur climbed back down to the rear of the cave where the wine was stored. He stooped down and quickly examined the pieces of broken pottery that littered the ground around his boots. Clumsy as they were, the dragons often broke the wine jugs with their wagging tails. Picking up the necks of some broken jugs, he fitted as many into his pockets as he could. Then he carefully climbed back up to his secret chamber.

Impatient with the delay, the dragons banged their clay goblets even harder on the ground and the whole cave echoed from the rhythmic sound.

"Where is Arthur?"

"What has happened to our wine?"

"We want wine. We want wine. We want wine!" shouted the dragons in unison.

"You want wine, eh?" Arthur whispered. "Well, you will get something you will never forget."

Like a little squirrel, Arthur carefully widened the openings in the walls of the cave with his fingernails and stuck the neck of a jug in each one. When he had finished placing the necks of the jugs all around the secret chamber, he carefully disguised his voice and started making noises at the dragons through the openings.

"Boooooooooh!" a deep, husky voice echoed down into the cave below. The dragons immediately hushed. There was no more banging of the goblets for wine.

"Boooooooooh!" Arthur continued. He went from opening to opening and shouted through his custom-made loudspeakers:

"Greedy, ruthless and foolish dragons! I have had enough of you! Unless you leave my forest this instant, I will slay you all, one by one!"

At first the dragons thought that the voices were some kind of joke, but when they couldn't figure out where the voices were coming from, fear began to sink in.

"Who are you?!" asked Ulof the Cunning, frantically looking around him.

""Show yourself. What do you want from us?"

"I am the woodland spirit that dwells in these woods," continued Arthur.

"Where is Arthur?" asked Drako the Invincible. "He never came back with the wine. Where is he when we need him most?"

"Is that his name?" replied the spooky voice from above. "*I* have your friend. He is my captive. I found him carrying your wine and I have imprisoned him behind these walls. Hear his cries."

Changing his voice back to normal, Arthur continued. "Help, my friends! Help me if you can, or run for your lives!"

"Yes, run for your lives you greedy, ruthless, and foolish dragons," echoed the voice through the openings in the ceiling. "Your friend will be the first to die, and then one by one it will be your turn," it threatened.

Arthur peeked through the openings and couldn't help laughing at what he saw down below.

Panic-stricken dragons were stumbling over each other like newborn chicks as they all ran towards the entrance of the cave.

Arthur decided to scare them even further. In the dimness of the cave, no one saw his dark shadow slipping by the walls.

Unnoticed by the dragons, Arthur grabbed his sword, put the goat cape over his head, and then rushed towards the central hearth. His shadow towered behind him, immediately rising all the way up to the ceiling and filling the walls of the cave, as tall as a mountain and as black as a crow. Raising his arms in order to intimidate and scare the dragons, Arthur moaned through his teeth in a deep, wild voice.

"Despicable dragons! Run for your lives, or by this blade you will perish one by one!" he cried, and tossed the sword from one hand to the other with the swiftness of a juggler tossing balls in a circus.

"The woodland spirit is playing tricks on our minds!" cried Ulof the Cunning. "One minute he talks behind the walls and the next he is here among us."

"Mercy! Mercy!" cried the dragons.

"Have pity on us, woodland spirit!"

"Push everybody! Push as hard as you can to get out of the cave."

But the spooked dragons, rushing all at once, quickly got stuck in the opening of the cave.

- 55 -

Arms and legs, bellies and heads all became one tangled mess!

"Get your foot off my eye, Drako," complained one.

"You're pulling my arm, Ulof!" shouted another.

"I can't breathe, Eli! Get your fat belly off me," yowled a third one.

Those who were not complaining pushed and squeezed even harder to get out of the cave, glancing fearfully back at the huge shadow creeping up behind them.

"The forest is all yours, woodland spirit!"

"And so is the cave!"

"We are leaving it to you. Our wine and food belong to you."

"Everything is yours, woodland spirit. Just spare our lives!"

Arthur's laughter echoed like thunder throughout the cave as the mass of bellies, jagged tails, arms and legs finally spilled out like an avalanche and rolled into the woods in one massive snowball, sweeping away trees and bushes along the way. Finally, the snowball exploded, sending trees, bushes, and dragons flying through the air. Those who survived the fall fled as far away as possible from the enchanted forest and its spooky woodland spirit.

A hero's return

That night, Arthur snuggled by the fire and enjoyed a deep, relaxing sleep, purring like a cat until dawn. The next morning, he woke up with a smirk on his face, satisfied with his accomplishments and amused by the events of the previous evening.

Having succeeded in his task, Arthur was ready to return to the village and claim his prize. He took up his sword, wrapped the goat cape around him, picked up his traveling cane, and left the cave whistling a happy tune. Despite the snow that lay thickly all around, he was able to identify the way back to the village by following the same features he had noticed on the way back from the raids: a bunch of bare trees, an eagle's nest, a fallen tree, a frozen spring, a steep cliff.

When he arrived at the village, all the villagers were out in the streets, talking loudly in small groups, too afraid to enter their homes. An earthquake struck their village the night before and nobody was able to sleep. The earthquake was so strong that all the pots fell from the shelves and the livestock got loose in the barns.

Arthur was immediately recognized by the two travelers who had taken him to the dragons. They ran up to him with open arms, hoping for good news, and soon the entire village gathered around them, all pushing and pulling in anticipation.

"Fear not, my friends!" announced Arthur. "No one is going to steal your livestock, take your wine, eat your vegetables, or eat your fruit without your permission. The forty dragons are gone. Last night's earthquake was nothing more than the crashing of their feet as they fled for their lives."

The villagers were so delighted with the news that they lifted Arthur high up on their shoulders in celebration and paraded him around the village with great cheers. It was an amusing parade of men, women, and children, followed by running geese, quacking ducks, and clucking chickens.

A huge feast was set up in the central square of the village to celebrate the defeat of the forty dragons. The villagers changed into their best clothes and sat down at an enormous table. As their guest of honor, Arthur was seated at the very center and devoured every delicacy that filled his plate. When his belly was full, Arthur joined the young boys and girls who danced around the fire holding hands. He was fascinated by the flames and hypnotized by the jingling sound of the jewelry and the golden coins that decorated the villagers' costumes.

All night long they danced around the fire and before they knew it, it was dawn! When Arthur looked up at the Three Sisters, he saw that an invisible artist was beginning to paint over the darkness of the sky.

A brushstroke of faint yellow slowly appeared behind the mountains. The twinkling stars faded one by one as the sun crowned the Three Sisters with its golden rays.

With the first light of day, the village elders approached Arthur and handed him his reward: a small chest filled with golden coins.

"Our beloved friend and fearless warrior, it would be a great honor if you would accept a place on our village council, and agree to take one of our beautiful young ladies as your wife," said the eldest as he gave Arthur a friendly tap on the shoulder.

Arthur blushed. The offers were tantalizing, but also embarrassing. The golden coins and the position on the council were most welcome, but marrying a local girl? No, no, no! He was far too young for marriage.

However, in time, he did fall in love with a young lady from the village and decided to marry her and settle down. His family traveled across the forest for the wedding. During the three-day festivities the blacksmith did not stop singing his son's praises, boasting with pride of Arthur's bravery and wit.

The sword

"**Do you remember the sword?**" asked Granny, making sure that her audience was not fast asleep from the warmth of the fireplace.

"Yes! Yes! We do!" shouted the grand-children, eager for more.

"Well, Arthur's sword was displayed at the entrance of the village, scaring off any thieves and scoundrels. For generations it hung over the main gate of the village."

At rest I slay forty. Beware when I rise!

"The story of the Fly-Slayer, who drove away the forty dragons, has been passed down from generation to generation around the fireplace."

"And all have lived happily ever after... Except for us," added Granny with a wink and a smile, testing her audience once more.

"No! No, Granny!"

"You are wrong!" corrected the children, giggling and laughing.

"For we will be even happier..."

Glossary

Acute: sharp, intense.

Anguished cry: a sharp, distressed cry showing suffering and pain.

Avalanche: a large mass of snow that detaches from a mountain slope and slides downhill.

Baffle: (verb) to confuse; puzzle; perplex.

Bandit: an outlaw; robber.

Bellow: (verb) to make a loud and deep animal cry.

Bobbin: a spool or a cylinder around which yarn or thread is wrapped.

Chamber: a private room; bedroom.

Clan: a large group of people or friends with common interests; a group of families who can trace their history to a common ancestor.

Cobblestone streets: streets paved with stones.

Commotion: noise with confusion and excitement.

Cunning: sly; tricky.

Deciduous trees: trees that shed their leaves in winter.

Despicable: worthless; detestable.

Dimness: lack of light; almost dark.

Disarray: lack of order; confusion.

Dispatch: (verb) to send away on a mission.

Dissuade: (verb) to discourage someone; talk him/her out of doing something; the opposite of persuade.

Dwell: (verb) to live; stay; reside; be housed.

Encounter: an unexpected meeting with someone.

Errand: a short and quick trip in order to do a job, often for somebody else.

Feeble: weak; faint; of little strength.

Flask: a water container, often made of dried animal skin.

Foe: an enemy; opponent; rival.

Goblet: a drinking cup with a tall stem.

Hearth: in this case, an outdoor fireplace with stones around it, where people gathered and danced.

Hides: animal skins used for making shoes or clothing.

In vain: to no end; without success or result.

Jagged tails: tails with uneven, zigzag points.

Loathsome: disgusting; sickening.

Mighty: very strong and courageous; of extraordinary power and size.

Oblivious: not aware of; showing no concern for what is happening around him/her.

Orchard: a piece of land planted with fruit or nut trees.

Perish: (verb) to die in a sudden way.

Praise: (verb) to express admiration or approval.

Quest: a search in order to find something; an adventurous journey.

Rear: the back part of something.

Scoundrel: a mean, bad person who deceives and cheats people.

Siblings: brothers and sisters, at least two people who have a common parent.

Slay: (verb) to kill by violence; kill by the sword.

Startle: (verb) to scare, frighten and surprise.

Swarm: (verb) to get together and/or move in large numbers, like bees gathering inside the beehive.

Symphony: a long piece of music written to be performed by an orchestra.

Tantalizing: tempting.

Task: a piece of work that is assigned and needs to be done; a duty.

Thatched roofs: roofs made of dry plants, such as straw, reeds, etc.

Tongs: a tool with two movable arms that are joined on one end and are used to hold or pick up objects.

Weary: very tired.

Wither: (verb) to become dry; decay; lose freshness.

Yawl: (verb) to howl; scream.

Maria Kamoulakou-Marangoudakis is an archaeologist and an award-winning children's author. She studied in England and holds two archaeology degrees. Maria's experience as a field archaeologist and a researcher with Greece's Hellenic Ministry of Culture spanned over sixteen years. Following her marriage to Carl, Maria moved to the USA in 2008 and decided to test her abilities in the sphere of children's literature.

© Photo Astro Klinakis

Her first book, *The Adventures of Hope & Trusty: Sky Cloud City*, is a fun adaptation of a classical Greek play, *The Birds*, by playwright Aristophanes. The story celebrates teamwork, brotherhood, friendship and peaceful coexistence. The Hope & Trusty adventure continues in an award-winning *Activity Book* that received *First Place* in the *2017 Purple Dragonfly Book Awards*. Both books have been translated into French and will soon be available by LITTLE CENTAUR PRESS.

Arthur the Fly-Slayer & the Forty Dragons is her second children's book. Maria wrote this story as a tribute to her father for his 90th birthday. It is based on a Spartan fairy tale that came down to her from her father's side of the family. When she is not busy writing children's stories, Maria enjoys interacting with her readers at book signing events and literary festivals. She is a wildlife lover and takes pleasure in attracting birds, particularly hummingbirds, and cottontail rabbits to her yard. Above everything else, Maria loves to travel, meet new people and learn about new cultures.

www.mariakamoulakou.com, mkamoulak@gmail.com

Born in Greece, **Ilias Sipsas** is a visual artist based in Athens. As an Art student, Ilias studied sculpture, marble crafting, photography and drawing. Occasionally he works for Greece's Hellenic Ministry of Culture as a marble craftsman and sometimes as a draftsman in archaeological sites all around Greece.

Arthur the Fly-Slayer & the Forty Dragons is Ilias's first ever children's book project. Every illustration is a mixed media collage of hand drawn sketches and watercolors, combined with elements from photographs and images from various sources. His goal is to create memorable, beautiful illustrations to be enjoyed by kids of all ages!

In the photo Ilias is four years old.

Acknowledgements

I would like to extend my deepest thanks and appreciation to: Ilias Sipsas for the beautiful and imaginative illustrations; Tanya Gold for her help with the developmental editing of the story; Pete Haddow for reading and editing the text; Allie Rottman, of *Silver Sparrow Editorial*, for proofreading the story; my beloved husband, Carl Marangoudakis, for reading my corrections over and over again; and my high school friend, Ina Melengoglou, of *Altsys Graphic Design*, for the amazing work she did with the layout of the book.